Howl like a wolf,
Buzz like a bee.
Then shout, with your own voice,
'Hello! This is me!'

Ian Larmont

My Big Band

'Ting' went the triangle.
'Foo' went the flute.
'Whee' went the whistle.
The horn went 'Toot'.

Whee

Foo

Tin

Toot

Crash

Boom

Ta-ra

Sounds Poems

Chosen by
John Foster

Contents

OXFORD

UNIVERSITY PRESS

Sounds Like Me

Roar like a lion,
Squeak like a mouse.
Miaow like a cat
Locked out of a house.

'Crash' went the cymbal.
'Boom' went the drum.
'Ta-ra' went the trumpet.
'Quiet!' yelled Mum.

Tony Mitton

Loud and Soft

YOU MUST SHOUT
IF I'M FAR AWAY
SO I CAN HEAR
WHAT YOU WANT TO SAY.

But if you and I
Are near
You can whisper
And I will hear.

Julie Holder

The Echo Bridge

There's an old bridge
Where I sometimes go,
If I stand underneath it
And shout 'Hello!'

'Hello, hello, hello,'
I hear the call,
Yet there's no one else there –
Just me, that's all.

I roar like a lion
And one roars back,
I howl like a wolf
And I hear the whole pack.

I growl like a tiger
And more growls come,
It feels so scary –
I run back home to Mum.

Daphne Lister

Footsteps

Boots tramp,
Wellies stamp,
Slippers slap,
Flip-flops flap,
Trainers squeak
On shiny floors.
Bare feet pad, pad, pad,
Like paws.

Julie Holder

13

Can You Hear?

The wind is a giant's breath,
I can hear him under my door.
He puffs and pants,
he moans and groans,
he whistles across my floor.

Judith Nicholls

On Rainy Days

The rain slaps and taps
against window panes.

The rain drops and plops
into puddles in lanes.

The rain giggles and gurgles
as it slurps down drains.

John Foster